BEES IN MY BUTT

Smartboys
Club #1

Rebecca Shelley

Illustrated by Abby Goldsmith

Wonder Realms Books

ISBN 978-1456599805

Text copyright © 2010 Rebecca Shelley
Illustrations copyright © 2011 Abby Goldsmith

Published by Wonder Realms Books

For Matthew who now WANTS
to be in the gifted program.

Smartboys Club

Book 1: Bees in My Butt

Book 2: We Flushed it Down the Potty

Book 3: I Took A Burp

Book 4: I Lost My Head

Book 5: My Stomach Explodes

Book 6: All I Got for Christmas

Chapter 1

The Bees Attack

Hi, my name's Monkey. Though my parents call me Johnny Lovebird. Lovebird, can you think of a worse name for a ten-year-old boy, I ask you?

Well I have to tell you, I'm a smart boy, and someday my teacher might discover the truth. I hope not anytime soon though. If she finds out how smart I am, she'll ship me off to the Gifted Program. Then I'll have to work, work, work, with no time left to spend with my friends, and no chance to learn all the interesting things I care about.

Yesterday she almost found out though. My troubles started at breakfast. First I got a squirmy wormy feeling in my gut and then . . .

Pppthffffffftthph!

Out it came like a swarm of bees, a fart so big even the neighbors down the street could hear it. Mom dropped her spoon and glared at me.

"Eeeeeew," my sister, Megan, screeched. She used to think passing gas was cool, but now she's in High School.

"Say excuse me," Dad ordered without looking up from his computer magazine.

I couldn't. I was laughing too hard and trying to hold my breath from the stink.

"Time out!" Mom pointed to the living room.

I abandoned my scrambled eggs and laughed all the way in there. The bees attacked three more times before I got to the couch. *Pft! Pft! Pft*! Boy did that smell bad. I sat in the stink and waited until my mom came in.

"Time to leave for school, Johnny. Why is your hair sticking up?" She licked her fingers and swiped at the back of my head.

I twisted away and grabbed my backpack. "Bye." I figured I'd get out before she gave me the lecture about passing gas at the table.

"Wait." Mom said. "Do you have any notes or papers for me from yesterday?"

I don't know why she always waits until the last second to look in my take-home folder. I mean, what if I had a note that said I had to bring ten dozen cookies that morning? Boy, she'd be in trouble.

She lifted the heavy backpack out of my hands. "Ugh, what have you got in here, a brick?" The zipper rasped open, and she reached in.

Uh-Oh. My face grew hot and my palms sweaty.

Mom pulled out a big fat book, *The Norton Anthology of English Literature*. "Hey, that's my college textbook. What are you doing with it?"

My mind spun, looking for an answer. The truth is, I'd been reading it, but I couldn't tell her that. "Well you see," I said, "we're pressing fall leaves in class, and I needed a big book to put them in."

"Oh." Frowning, she opened the book to the place I had marked.

No leaves.

"Gotta go, Mom." I grabbed the book and shoved it into my pack. My hand brushed hers as she pulled out my homework folder. I rubbed my sweaty palms on my jeans and edged toward the door while she flipped through it.

"Johnny." Her eyes riveted on my multiplication test. "You missed every question on this. What kind of answers are these? Since when does eight times six equal one point three?"

"Um, I felt kind of sick yesterday." This was bad. I tried to get outside, but she grabbed my arm.

"Wait a minute." Mom's forehead wrinkled. "You divided all these numbers instead of multiplying?"

Busted.

Actually I'd made them into improper fractions, then divided to get a mixed number and converted that into decimal form—all in my head of course—and finished long before the timer went off.

Abandoning my homework folder, I raced out the door, my heart pounding, my feet churning across the lawn. I couldn't help playing with the math. Mrs. Red keeps making us do the same dumb times-table drills over and over again. I had to do something to make them interesting.

I ran down the street to Bean's house. Bean is my best friend. His name is really Tommy Jones, but we call him Bean because he loves math. He says people who are good at numbers are called bean counters. Anyway, Bean stood on the sidewalk out front waiting for me. "Hey, Monkey. What took you so long?"

I doubled over, panting. "Mom got hold of my folder. I'm in trouble. She figured out what I did on the times-table test."

"Hmm," Bean said, staring back toward my house. The wind ruffled his short white-blond hair. I wish my hair were blond like that. Mine's just dirty brown-blond to match my brown eyes. At least I'm taller than Bean. That's got to count for something.

"Maybe she'll forget about it by the end of the day," Bean said. "Remember, she sometimes forgets where she's going by the time she gets halfway out of the driveway."

I laughed. Maybe Bean was right. Mom is forgetful. Still I worried.

Bean started walking toward school. "Hey, isn't your mom supposed to be at the Family Fitness Center for water aerobics in the morning. What's she doing home?"

I shrugged. "She and her friends started taking another class later on. Don't know what. You should see the bruise she has on her knuckles though. Big green circle. She said she hit her fist on something."

Bean shook his head. "You've got a great mom, Monkey. My mom is too busy correcting papers for her university students to look at my work. Good thing too. She never notices when I do interesting stuff on my math papers." He hitched up his backpack and kicked a rock down the sidewalk in front of us.

Thinking about my mom and my math quiz made my gut hurt. *Pft. Pft. Pft.* The bees came swarming out again.

Bean wrinkled his nose.

"*Phffft!*" I faked the sound then laughed to hide my embarrassment. But that was just the beginning.

Chapter 2

The Smartboys Club

Bean and I reached Chrom-El just as the bell rang. That's short for Chromatic Elementary. Of course the school's real name is Rainbow Elementary. It's a big building made with red bricks, and it has colored tiles over the front entryway that make a rainbow. Anyway, chromatic is a neat sounding word for color. Why use a boring word like rainbow when you could say chromatic? Just my opinion. I love words and books.

Bean and I waved to Tom Brown, the janitor, as we headed inside. Tom waved back and called for us to hurry or we'd be late. We rushed to our room and sat down. Our class is divided into three groups. The teacher's favorite kids sit on the right side. The average kids sit on the left. The rest of us sit in the back.

"Roll Call," Mrs. Red said. She's our teacher. She's really old, like twenty-eight years, and she keeps her hair pulled back in an elastic, which makes her face look like a horse.

Bbbffpptbbffpptbbffppt!

Everyone knew I was there and wished I wasn't.

"Excuse me," I chirped before Mrs. Red could protest my bodily outburst. What a smell.

While Mrs. Red took the roll, Bean crawled toward the pencil sharpener. I gave him a low-five under the desk as he passed. One of these days he's going to make it all the way to the sharpener and back without getting caught. Then he's going to try for the drinking fountain.

Vinny says he should just raise his hand and ask to go sharpen his pencil, but what's the fun of that?

Oh, Vinny's our friend. You see, Bean and I started a Smartboys Club for everyone who finished their math workbooks the first week of school. Of course that was just him and me. And . . . except . . . well Vinny did too.

She's a girl. Virginia Garcia Diaz. She finished even faster than we did, and she can speak two languages, Spanish and English. Besides that, she's a whiz on the computer. We had to let her into the club.

Poor Vinny. The teacher found out about the math workbook and gave her another, harder one. That's why Bean and I keep this sort of thing secret.

Then there's Art. His real name is Kyung-sam Gee. He's still working on his math from third grade. But we let him in because he makes a basket almost every time he shoots the ball, and he can draw spaceships and robots and dinosaurs better than Mrs. Lavender, the art teacher. I guess it's obvious why we call him Art. He even has an uncle in the city who is a famous artist. Oh, and he speaks Korean too. I wish my parents spoke a different language so I could learn one like Art and Vinny.

Bbbffppt. The bees in my butt speak a language all their own.

"Peeew," Bean said. He was on the floor by my desk, right in line with the blast.

Art made a pretend fart and spit all over his desk.

Vinny turned around to glare at him. "Guh-ross!"

"Tommy, get back in your seat and be quiet," Mrs. Red said.

"Hey, I didn't," Bean complained. "I was just going to sharpen my pencil." But Mrs. Red wrote his name on the white board.

If you get your name up there, that's a warning. If you get a check mark by it, you have think-time for five minutes in the little desk out in the hall. If you get another mark, you have to stay in from recess.

I don't know why Mrs. Red bothers to erase our names off the board everyday after school. Bean and Art and I. She might as well leave them up there.

Bean says having our names on the board hides our secret identity as members of the Smartboys Club. Vinny sits on the right side of the room with the teacher's favorite students. She has her own secret identity. She pretends to be a good student even though she's really a member of our club.

Bean returned to his seat next to me. "So what's up with the farting?" he whispered.

"I don't know," I answered. "I think I must have been sleepwalking last night and swallowed a whole beehive or something. I got the pesky things flying around all through my guts and bursting out like crazy. Who knew bees could smell so bad?"

"Hmmm," Bean said, getting out his English workbook and propping it up on his desk so Mrs. Red couldn't see what he was doing.

I got mine out as well and started the morning work.

Bean pulled his cell phone from his pocket. Keeping it hidden behind his workbook, he linked to the Internet. He says you can find the answer to almost anything online. Of course you have to cross-check the research to make sure it's correct.

A moment later he had a medical website up.

"Flatulence, also known as gas, is air in the intestines that passed out through the rectum." Bean wrinkled his nose at me as a prime example of flatulence burst out.

"Intestine and rectum," Art said, "what are those?"

"Art, if you didn't play basketball so well, we'd have to kick you out of the club," I said. "Intestine is your gut and rectum is the doctor's word for butt."

Bean clicked to the next page and continued. "Gas is formed in the intestines by digesting foods. It can create bloating and cramps. That's your bees, Monkey."

"Okay," I said. "So how did I get this stuff?"

"Better question. Is it catchable?" Art asked.

"Of course it's not contagious," Bean said. "Gas is caused by swallowing air while eating, or eating foods that are hard to digest. What did you have for dinner last night, Monkey?"

"Taco salad and burritos." I rubbed my tummy and licked my lips. I love Mexican food.

"That'll do it," Bean said.

Pftpftpftpfptfptpftpftfptffffftt!

"That does it for me," Art yelled, abandoning his seat next to mine.

Bean followed him up to Mrs. Red's desk. "Can we sit somewhere else today?"

Boy did I feel lucky to have friends like that. Not!

Chapter 3

Storm Clouds

The bell rang for recess. Art left his workbook out on his desk to cover the scene of a t-rex fighting a triceratops that he'd drawn on his desktop. He grabbed his basketball and bolted out the door. While Mrs. Red wasn't looking, I slipped the *Norton Anthology* out of my backpack, and Bean got his portable weather station and notebook.

Outside, the wind blew cold, scratching the brown leaves across the asphalt. My gut still hurt. I followed Bean over to the basketball standard where Art dribbled the ball, aimed, and shot. The ball *thumped* against the backboard and whooshed down through the hoop.

"Hana," Art cried, retrieving the ball. That's the word for *one* in Korean. I think he's reached twenty-five baskets in a row before without missing.

I sat down, crossed my legs, and opened the anthology in my lap. Bean set up his little blue weather station and wrote down the temperature. The cups on the anemometer spun around faster and faster. Vinny joined us, fighting to keep her long black hair from blowing in her face. She frowned at the cell phone in her hand.

Thump. "Dool," Art shouted. Two baskets.

"The air pressure is dropping, and those are cumulonimbus clouds," Bean said, pointing at the line of billowing black clouds moving across the sky toward us. "Looks like a thunderstorm."

I rubbed my hands across the book's dusty old pages, anxious to get back to the story about the great warrior, Beowulf. But Vinny frantically punched buttons on her phone.

"What's wrong, Vinny?" I asked.

"My Dad's supposed to be on instant messaging right now. But he's not there." Vinny fingered her grandmother's wedding ring that she has worn since her grandmother's funeral. She tends to play with the ring when she's nervous.

I set my book aside and went over to her. Her dad's in the army, and she worries about him. "I'm sure he's fine, Vinny. Maybe something's wrong with your instant messaging." Her dark brown eyes stared straight at me for a second. Then she looked down at the phone.

"Sí. That's it."

I went back to my book while she started trouble-shooting her program.

Thump. "Set." Three baskets.

"Hey, Monkey," Bean said. "Did you finish your reading comprehension homework?"

"Of course." I scanned down through the thick jumble of words to where Beowulf wrestled with the monster, Grendel, and tore Grendel's arm off. Cool.

"But I didn't see you turn it in," Bean said while checking the thermometer.

Thump. "Net." Four baskets.

"Oh no." My heart did a flip-flop. Thunder rumbled in the sky. "I left my homework in the folder with my mom," I cried.

Bean shook his head in disbelief.

I fumbled my cell phone out of my pocket and dialed my phone number. Technically we're allowed cell phones at school as long as they're turned off during class.

A busy signal pulsed in my ear. Strange, my mom hates talking on the phone.

"Yes," Vinny crowed. "I got him. He's on now!"

Art looked at Vinny just as he shot. *Kathump.* The ball karoomed off the rim instead of going in. He'd have to start over, but he gave Vinny a thumbs up.

I'd have been happier for her if bees weren't swarming through my gut, and I could get my mom to bring my homework to school. I closed the phone and slid it back into my pocket.

Pbbffttt! I farted just as a crack of thunder sounded overhead.

Art dribbled the ball and shot again. Vinny chatted online with her dad, and Bean recorded the weather in his notebook. Tuning out my friends and ignoring the bees, I focused on Beowulf. What an incredible story. Beowulf had defeated Grendel, but Grendel's mother showed up and captured one of Beowulf's friends. Beowulf chased her to a big lake, dove in, and fought her. His sword bounced off her thick skin.

I bit my lip. There seemed like no escape for Beowulf. Then he saw an old sword, made by giants. Jewels glittered in the handle. He grabbed it and thrust it through the monster.

She screamed, *aaaahhhhhrrrriiiiinnnnnggg*!

"Monkey, that's the bell." Bean shook me.

I gasped. The bell, not a scream. Of course. I stood up, and the bees burst from my butt again. The smell of those could have killed a monster.

I closed the book and dialed my mom one more time, hoping to reach her. The phone rang and rang and rang. I frowned. She couldn't be gone. It wasn't time for her class at the fitness center, and she was just there talking on the line a few minutes ago. More rings. Still no answer.

Thunder rumbled. "Come on," Bean yelled. "Let's get inside. The last thing we want is to get wet."

Chapter 4

F-A-R-T-I-N-G

As soon as we got inside, Mrs. Red told us to line up at the door. "We have an assembly today," she said, clapping her hands for us to hurry. The right side of the room walked to the door in a quiet line. The left side of the room whooped and dove for the door, butting in front of the right side.

"What sort of assembly?" Bean said, returning his weather station to the back corner inside his desk.

I joined Vinny in line at the door. My stomach felt snakey.

"This will be our annual assembly where the 5th and 6th graders review the school rules and motto," Mrs. Red told the class. "Now get in line, Tommy."

Bean sighed and got in line behind me and Art.

"Who can tell me the three B's of our school motto?" Mrs. Red asked before opening the door.

"Be happy. Be hungry. Be hip!" I shouted to cover the sound of the bees popping from my butt.

Vinny, Art, and Bean backed away from me, holding their noses.

Mrs. Red frowned at me. "Not quite."

"Be smart. Be active. Believe," Bean said.

"Be creative. Be swift. Be better than anyone else," Art said.

"NO!" Mrs. Red pressed her hands against her ears and shook her head. She has never liked all our creative answers to that question.

We fell silent.

The stink from the bees hung around me.

"Bridget, would you please tell us the school motto?" Mrs. Red asked the girl with the long blond hair. Bridget is Mrs. Red's favorite student.

Bridget folded her arms and glared smugly at us Smartboys. "Be safe. Be responsible. Be respectful."

"Yes, thank you." Mrs. Red opened the door and led the class down the hall to the gym.

Eric Dripp, the curly-haired boy in front of Vinny, turned toward me. "Johnny Lovebird sitting in a tree F-A-R-T-I-N-G."

I tried to hit him, but Vinny caught me and kept me in line. "Smartboys don't need to pay attention to losers like Eric," she whispered in my ear.

My face burned. I HATE that Lovebird song.

We passed the front office. Probably a dozen moms stood out in the hall between it and the gym. I supposed they were 5th and 6th grade moms who'd come to see their kids do the assembly. I recognized some of them as my mom's friends.

One mom with a pinched, white face and spiky, brown hair had a corner of black fabric sticking out of her purse. She saw me looking at it and stuffed it back in quick-like then gave me a glare.

I let off a good one as I passed her. If you've gotta have gas, might as well use it.

In the gym we sit in rows all scrunched together. Hundreds of kids close enough we can smell each other's bad breath. I sat with Eric and Vinny on one side of me and Art and Bean on the other. A whole row of third-graders squashed in front of us and a row of fourth-graders right behind.

Principal Green stood at the front of the auditorium on the stage steps. "Welcome everyone. I'm so glad you're here and blah blah blah. . . ."

My gut hurt. The bees swarmed fit to kill a bear stealing their honey. They buzzed for freedom, and I fought to keep them in.

The fifth-graders started their silly skit where they pretended to walk through the halls, breaking every school rule. They pushed and shoved, ran and did cartwheels. Someone even scribbled on the wall.

"Stop!" the kid pretending to be the principal screamed. "That is wrong, wrong, wrong! Go back to your classroom and try again." The fifth-graders returned to the front of the gym and lined up quietly.

My stomach pressed against the top of my pants, making me feel like I'd just eaten a huge Thanksgiving feast. My gut grumbled and mumbled. I sat up straight and tight. Not here, I thought, please not here with the whole school to smell it.

The fifth-graders finished demonstrating perfect hall behavior. Then the lights dimmed, and the big screen lowered in front of the stage. The sixth-graders started a PowerPoint presentation about proper behavior on the playground, using pictures they had taken of students during recess.

Bean grabbed my arm. "Hey, that's us."

We were sitting against the school's red brick wall reading a comic book. He and I both knew we'd been using the comic book as a cover while we tried to figure out an algebra book Bean had "borrowed" from his older brother.

Now I'm good at math, but that book was hard.

Bean said he understood it, but I didn't believe him.

My stomach twisted into a tighter knot. I tried to catch Mrs. Red's eye so I could ask to go to the bathroom. At least everyone expected the bathroom to stink to high heaven.

"Reading is not proper playground behavior," one of the sixth-graders said into the mic. "Everyone needs to run and play and get exercise."

All the kids laughed. Eric made a crazy sign by his head and pointed at Bean and me.

My cheeks burned hot, and I clenched my fists, glaring at Eric. Bean growled under his breath. I couldn't believe the sixth-grader said that. We should be able to do whatever we want for recess, and our parents and teachers keep saying how important it is to read.

The PowerPoint moved on, but I kept thinking about that picture.

The bees in my butt grew ferocious, ready to swarm out all over everyone. Since Mrs. Red wasn't looking at me, I snatched my cell phone out of my pocket and text messaged the other Smartboys.

Art, Bean, and Vinny whipped out their phones to see what I'd sent.

Hold your noses. It's going to blow.

Vinny dropped her phone and grabbed for her nose. Bean and Art managed to slip their phones back in their pockets before readying for the big bang. I gave up trying to hold it in. If everyone was going to make fun of us for reading on the playground, then they'd get what they deserved.

PPPPPpftpftpftpfptfptpftpftfptffffftttppthffffffftthph!!!

Chapter 5

Ninjas

My fart echoed through the whole gym. The stink nearly knocked me unconscious. Chaos filled the auditorium like the world's biggest explosion. The kids around us screamed and scrambled to get away. The sixth-graders stopped their presentation and pinched their noses.

Mrs. Green yelled into the mic. "Everyone sit down! Teachers, open the doors and windows!" Her face turned an ugly shade of green to match her name.

I sat in the middle of all the madness. The other Smartboys stayed with me, still holding their noses, of course.

"Ah," I said, rubbing my tummy. "That's much better."

"Speak for yourself," Vinny said. Her voice came out funny because of her pinched nose. "Monkey, you've got serious medical problems."

Bean shook his head. "No, we already looked it up. It's not life threatening."

"It's not?" Art said, staring at the sick-looking faces around them. "I bet everyone here thinks they're going to die."

"Hey, Lovebird," Eric yelled. "You know weapons aren't allowed in school." He gave me an evil grin and fanned his hand in front of his face.

"Neither are dogs," I yelled back at him. "Your owners should keep you on a leash."

"That's enough!" the principal shouted. "Everyone get back in your seats now."

"We don't have seats," Vinny called. "We've gotta sit on the floor like a herd of cows, remember?"

Fortunately for Vinny the principal couldn't hear her because of the noise. But she shouldn't risk exposing her secret identity as a good kid to say that. Poor Vinny. Sometimes what she thinks just comes popping out of her mouth before she can stop it.

The teachers got the gym doors open. There were no windows, of course. A ball would break them, wouldn't it? Not that Principal Green spends enough time in the gym to pay attention to that type of thing.

While everyone worked their way back to their seats, a black shadow flitted in the front door and crept close to the stage where Principal Green and the sixth-graders stood.

I twisted my head around to see the other doors. A chill went up my spine. A horde of black-clad people snuck into the gym. Black masks covered their faces. In the chaos caused by my explosion, no one but me seemed to notice. They fanned out, surrounding us, silent shadows, moving like liquid.

I poked Bean and pointed to the invaders.

"Ninjas," Bean said in awe. "Why would they come here?"

Who knew, but I counted twelve of them, all carrying red water-blasters. They eased the doors shut and locked them. Then stood motionless, waiting.

One of them leaped up the stage steps to Principal Green and the sixth-graders. This one had a red headband and all the others just wore black. She had to be their leader. She did a flying side kick across the stage, knocking the mic out of Principal Green's hands. That got everyone's attention.

Cries of surprise and fear rose up from the teachers and students.

"Who are you? What are you doing here?" Principal Green said, glaring at them. "It is against the rules to bring weapons to school, and that includes water guns. Hand them over and go straight to my office."

Ignoring her, the lead ninja lifted the microphone from the floor. "Everyone stay where you are, stay calm, and nobody gets wet."

"Ha, I bet those things aren't even loaded," one of the sixth-graders said.

A stream of water pumped from the leader's water-blaster, soaking him.

Principal Green, raised her hands over her head. "Stop, don't do anything rash. I wore my blue silk shirt today. It's dry-clean only. Just tell me what you want." My jaw dropped. So much for Principal Green saving us.

"We are the Majestic Order for Modern Schools," the ninja shouted into the mic. "We don't like the way the school district is running this elementary. As of today, we're taking over and making this a charter school."

"Charter school?" I muttered.

Vinny leaned over to whisper in my ear. "Charter schools are run by parent committees. My mom tried to get me into one before the start of this school year, but there's a really long waiting list because so many parents want their kids to go to the charter school instead of here."

Vinny folded her arms and sat back. "Maybe things will get better around here. I bet they'll force everyone to do their best."

Bean and I looked at each other. Better? That didn't sound like such a good idea to us.

Chapter 6

Better and Better

"You can't take over," Principal Green whined. "I'm in charge here."

A spray of water burst from the gun and hit her right in the face. "No. We're in charge here. We've cut the phone lines and locked the gate to the parking lot. Don't even think of resisting."

Principal Green blinked the water out of her eyes. "You'll regret this."

"Maybe we will," one of the ninjas said, "but these children will get the kind of education they deserve."

One of the ninjas saw Vinny's cell phone lying on the floor where she'd dropped it.

The ninja did a backflip over the crowd, landed next to Vinny, and snatched up the phone. "Naughty, naughty. Electronic devices are no longer allowed in this school." She pocketed the phone and put her hands on her hips, glaring at Vinny. Of course it's hard to glare well in a mask that covers your face.

Vinny glared back, but kept quiet.

I was glad my phone was hidden away.

"Now everyone back to your classrooms," the lead ninja said into the mic. Her voice boomed out across the gym. "We'll waste no more time on useless assemblies. School is a place for learning, not playing."

"Line up!" she shouted. Her voice sounded sort of familiar, but the mask muffled it. I didn't know any ninjas anyway, so I figured I just imagined it.

Everyone stared at her in disbelief.

She raised her hand. "When I give an order, you will follow it instantly, or else." Another ninja appeared at her side, holding a thick board. The lead ninja drew her hand back, made a fist, and smashed the board, breaking it in half.

The kids gasped and scrambled into lines at the doors.

"Wow?" Bean said.

I shuddered and rubbed my fist. "That's got to hurt."

"Not really," Art said. "It only hurts if you don't break the board." Art knows these things. I think he's done just about every sport there is.

We lined up with our class. To my surprise, the lead ninja marched over to take us back to our room. As soon as we sat down she said. "Clear your desks. We'll start by taking an assessment test to see how much you've learned so far."

Mrs. Red tried to protest and got a spray of water up her nose.

The ninja got Bridget to carry the tests while she came down the aisle, plopping one on each person's desk. She held her red water-blaster in her free hand, ready to use. The tests were so huge, they rumbled like an earthquake when they hit the desks.

Art left his English notebook on his desk and fumbled through his pencil box for an eraser. He wasn't fast enough.

The ninja paused with test in hand, hovering over Art's desk. "I said clear your desks."

Art eased the workbook off his desk, revealing his magnificent picture beneath.

The ninja screeched in outrage and soaked Art with a blast of water. "Clean if off!" she screamed.

Art set to work with the eraser.

"Fifty extra push-ups for you, young man." She slammed the test onto his desk and moved on.

Once we all had our tests, she stood at the front of the room, cradling the gun in her arms. "When I say go, you will start. There will be no talking. No cheating. And anyone who doesn't do their very best is going to pay."

She snapped a roundhouse kick across Mrs. Red's desk, sending the pencil holder shooting across the room. It slammed into the wall and rattled to the floor. I shuddered.

"That includes you, Johnny Lovebird," she said pointing a wicked black-gloved finger at me, "and you too, Tommy Jones. I know you've been hiding behind a thin veil of stupidity. As of today, that stops."

I gasped. How could she know our true identities?

Chapter 7

The Test

The test started easy, with kindergarten stuff— shapes and colors, letters and numbers. Vinny glared at the paper in disbelief. "You call this a test?" she said, but a bell rang just as she said it, so the ninja didn't hear.

I chuckled and started working.

Things changed quickly though, going to addition and subtraction and then multiplication and division and fractions. No sweat. Then the numbers started getting jumbled with letters like they had been in Art's brother's algebra book.

Bean's pencil flew across the paper.

I frowned at him. We both know I'm the smarter one.

I glanced up and found the ninja's squirt gun pointed right at my nose. "Keep going," the ninja said, "and no funny business."

I took a deep breath. It couldn't be that hard. The book had said the letters stand for missing numbers. You use the numbers you do know, to figure out the numbers you don't. Okay.

My hand shook, but I solved every math question and then moved on to the reading part of the test and then the spelling and grammar. At least those were easy.

Bean finished twenty minutes before me. That made me mad, and I worked harder.

Art was still stuck on the first half of the test when the lunch bell rang.

Vinny leaned back in her chair and smiled. I dropped my pencil on my desk. "What are you smiling about?" I mouthed to her.

She pointed at my rear. "No bees," she mouthed back.

She was right. I'd been so focused on the test and not being outdone by Bean, I hadn't even noticed that the bees had gone into hibernation. I could feel them snoring away in there, but none had tried to escape for a while.

"Time's up," the ninja said. "Line up for lunch."

"Hey," Mrs. Red said. "It's my job to say 'line up for lunch.'"

"Not anymore," the ninja said. "I just got word from the ninja committee. You don't equal up to their teaching requirements. You're fired, Mrs. Red."

"No!" the right half of the class protested.

"Things are going downhill fast," Bean whispered to me. We both liked Mrs. Red. Any other teacher might have figured out about the Smartboys Club by now.

"You can't fire me," Mrs. Red said. "The school district would have to do that."

"The district is no longer in charge. We are." The ninja squirted Mrs. Red in the ear.

We all lined up at the door.

I thought about my own red water-blaster at home, and wished I had it. Then at least the fight would be even. But no, I was stuck at the school weaponless against a bunch of crazed ninjas.

And as soon as they corrected my test, they'd have proof that I was a Smartboy.

My easy life would end. They'd put me in the Gifted Program. I wanted to scream in frustration. I'd have to go to a different school and leave behind my friends and everything else that was really important to me.

My stomach did a flip-flop and woke up the bees.

Chapter 8

The Smartest Boy

We walked down the hall toward the lunch room. The school smelled funny, and I wondered what they had cooked for lunch. Bean grabbed my arm and pointed out the doors to the first and second graders at lunch recess. The ninjas had them lined up in the rain, doing jumping jacks and push-ups. No playing.

Art gasped. "What about basketball? They can't take away recess."

I gritted my teeth. I'd left Beowulf at the bottom of the lake and wanted to get back to the story.

Bean shook his head. "This is bad."

We passed the gym and saw a ninja forcing a sixth grade class to do ballet for physical education. Vinny stifled a laugh. Some of the boys and girls looked terribly ungraceful.

"That is just sick and wrong," Art said.

"Actually," Bean whispered. "Ballet is an excellent form of exercise and conditioning. But I'd rather play dodgeball any day."

As soon as we reached the lunch room, I figured out what smelled so bad. The ninjas had taken over the kitchen and cooked broccoli, Brussels sprouts, and tofu salad. I lifted my tray of gross food with shaking hands.

This was definitely not going to help my flatulence. I needed something smooth and easy like ice cream to digest.

A sickening quiet filled the lunchroom. The ninjas stood around the tables, squirting anyone who banged their silverware, burped, or talked too loud. On the way to our table, we heard one of the third graders whisper that the ninjas had shut down all the computers in the computer lab and declared it off limits for safety reasons.

Vinny dropped her tray, and tofu salad flew everywhere. A Brussels sprout bounced up and hit the third grader in the back of the head.

The third grader yelped. A blast of water shot through the air from one of the ninja's guns, soaking Vinny. "Clean that mess up this instant, young lady," the ninja ordered.

Vinny bent to it, and the rest of us put our trays on the table and came back to help. What a mess. While we worked, we couldn't help overhearing more whispers. The ninjas had doubled everyone's homework, taken the doors off the stalls in the bathroom, and cancelled the science fair. Good thing Bean wasn't holding a tray of food when he heard that one. His face turned bright red.

"Monkey," he whispered as we walked to our table. His voice shook. "We've got to do something."

"I agree." Vinny slumped onto the bench and fingered her grandmother's ring. "I was wrong. The ninjas are ruining the school."

I grimaced. They all looked at me to come up with some kind of a plan, and all I could think about was that test the ninja had given us. I'd done way too well. Bean had too, but he didn't seem worried about it.

I poked at my food. "We have a more serious problem."

"We do?" Bean said, stabbing a Brussels sprout like it was trying to climb off the plate and bite his hand.

I dropped my fork and glared at him. "That ninja knows our secret identities. She made us take that test just so she could prove how smart we really are. As soon as she corrects the tests, we're doomed!"

Bean's face twisted up into a weird grimace, and his eyes crossed. He always makes that face when he thinks I've said or done something really stupid.

"Monkey, you didn't actually fill in the right answers did you?"

"You mean you didn't?" My heart skipped a beat.

Bean snorted. "Of course not. I used the numbers from Pi to fill in the answers, so it looked like I was trying to do the problems not just guessing or doing them wrong on purpose."

"Pie? Sounds yummy," Art said. He paused in his creation of a food statue. He'd stacked pieces of tofu to make a dinosaur with a Brussels sprout head.

Bean made his stupid face again. "Pi is the ratio of the circumference of a circle to its diameter."

Art's eyes bugged out. "The what?"

Vinny patted Art's arm. "Pi is a mucho long number that goes on forever and never repeats itself. Bean used the part of Pi he has memorized to fill in the answers."

I sucked in a quick breath. "Bean, you really are smarter than I am."

Bean chuckled. "Of course."

"But you run the chance of someone recognizing the numbers as Pi," I said. "Just like my mom figured out what I did on yesterday's math quiz."

Bean choked on his tofu.

"Not likely," he said when he'd stopped coughing. "Why would a bunch of ninjas have Pi memorized? Most people can't get past 3.14." I knew he was right. Still that wouldn't save me. My worries woke the bees. They buzzed through my gut and burst out. *Pft-pft-pft-ptffffffttt!*

Three sprays of water hit me from the ninjas' guns.

I said, "excuse me," too late.

Now I was dripping wet and feeling stupid. I should have thought of something like that Pi trick.

"What am I going to do?" I said. "Once they correct that test, I'm a goner."

Chapter 9

Busted

"I've got an idea." Art added lettuce to his dinosaur's back to make it a stegosaurus.

"What?" I was desperate.

"I saw the ninja take the tests into the Teachers' Lounge with her. If we can get the ninjas and teachers out, you can sneak in and put your name on Eric's test and his name on yours."

"Great idea," Bean said. "They can ship Eric off to the Gifted Program, and you'll stay here with us."

"How are we going to get the teachers and ninjas out of the lounge?" Vinny asked.

I smiled. The bees swarmed around in my gut. "Leave that to me."

We dumped our trays and pretended to head outside for the required jumping jacks and push-ups. While a ninja squirted a boy who didn't move fast enough, we snuck down the hall toward the lounge instead. On the way, we passed the library.

I stopped.

A squad of ninjas pulled books off the shelves and stacked them on a big cart.

"*Harry Potter*," one of them said, dropping the heavy book on the cart like it had burned her hand. "We can't have the kids reading anything like that."

"True," another ninja said. "We need to keep their minds firmly in reality."

"I like *See Spot Run*," the first said.

The ninjas all agreed to that one.

"*Captain Underpants*?" one asked.

The other ninjas screamed and dove for the shelf that held all the *Captain Underpants* books. They went onto the cart faster than you can snap your fingers. Other books followed.

Bean, Vinny, and Art noticed I'd stopped and turned back to stare at me.

"Th-they can't," I stammered, pointing to the ninjas in the library. "We have to stop them."

"That's what I said at lunch," Bean whispered. "Now do you believe me?"

I nodded. My face burned, and my heart raced. No science fair. No recess. No computers. Fine. But take away my books, and just like Colonel Travis at the Alamo, that's where I draw the line.

The ninjas pushed the cart out the door, and we scattered so they wouldn't see us. Vinny and Art dove into the girls bathroom. Bean and I jumped into the lost and found bin with all the coats and gloves.

The cart's wheels squeaked as the ninjas pushed it down the hall and around the corner.

I peeked out. "Coast is clear," I whispered.

The others joined me.

An idea came to me. "Come on," I said.

We scurried after the cart and turned the corner just in time to see it go outside.

"Somebody do something," Vinny cried.

Bean grabbed Art's arm and dragged him out the door. Vinny and I followed. We ran around the side of the school so we could get a clear look at the ninjas trundling the cart down the hill toward the dumpster.

"What now?" I said.

Bean grabbed a baseball-sized rock from the ground. "This calls for the use of mass and momentum." He handed the rock to Art. "Throw this so it lands right in front of the cart's wheels."

Art looked at him like he was crazy.

"Do it," Bean said. "Everyone else get ready to run for the books."

Art wound up and pitched the rock. It thudded to the ground directly in front of the cart.

CRASH! The cart's wheels struck the rock and stopped turning. The sudden stop sent all the books flying into the air. They tumbled to the ground in a huge mess.

"Now!" I yelled and sprinted for the books.

I grabbed all the *Captain Underpants* books. Bean grabbed as many *Harry Potter* books as he could carry. Art snatched up the *Doctor Seuss* books, and Vinny dove for the *Dragon Codex* books.

The ninjas turned their squirt guns on us and soaked our backs as we ran as fast as we could into the school.

"Stop!" the ninjas yelled, chasing us.

"What now?" Bean said, his feet pumping to try to keep ahead of the ninjas.

I skidded to a stop in front of the lost-and-found box and dumped my armload of books inside. The others did the same. We arranged it super fast so that the coats were on top, then closed the lid and dashed farther down the hall.

"Freeze!" The ninjas came around the corner and saw us. Their guns pointed straight at us. As wet as I already was, I figured I shouldn't have bothered taking a shower that morning.

"Where are the books?" the ninjas demanded.

I held up my hands. "I don't know. They just magically vanished."

The ninjas' eyes went buggy. "You four are in big trouble. We're taking you straight to our leader."

"Oh, please don't. Anything but that," I pleaded.

The ninjas cackled with laughter and pushed us down the hall toward the Teachers' Lounge.

Chapter 10

Failure

In the lounge, teachers and ninjas crowded the round tables and stood at the counter. The microwave dinged, and the smell of warm popcorn drifted out.

Everyone stared as our captors marched us into the room.

Principal Green sat at the far table. Her face was white and her left eye twitched. She took a sip from a bottled water that must have come from the cases of them piled up beside the refrigerator. Her blue silk shirt had ugly, dark water spots all over it.

The ninja leader jumped to her feet. Ninjas sat on either side of her with red pens in their hands. Our tests were on the table in front of them.

"What's going on?" the lead ninja demanded.

"These four stole some books." One of the ninjas shoved my shoulder with her gun.

"Johnny Lovebird!" the lead ninja hollered. "You stole something?"

The ninja's voice made my skin crawl it was so familiar.

I raised my hand. "Um . . . I prefer to be called Monkey. And, we didn't really steal the books. They were going out to the dumpster anyway."

"It's outrageous," Vinny chimed in. "Throwing away literary classics just because you don't understand them."

Yes, Vinny never could keep herself from speaking her mind at the worst moments.

"Silence!" the lead ninja said. "You four will return the books at once, and then spend the rest of the day in think-time writing me an essay on why it is wrong to steal."

Art and Bean groaned.

It was time to make my move.

I let loose a swarm of bees that were sure to blow the doors off.

PFFPHTTHPPTHBUBUBPUUFFFPHTH!!!!!!!!!!!

Rotten-egg-smelling-stink filled the room. I pinched my nose and stepped aside as the teachers and ninjas stampeded from the room. I ran to the table where the tests were and spread them out, looking for mine. I found it. Not a red mark on it.

Bean grabbed Eric's test. Red pen covered it.

"Quick, erase the names," Bean said.

I froze. "I don't have an eraser." I didn't have a pencil either, to rewrite the names.

"Oh no, they'll be back pronto," Vinny said.

"Just a second." Art reached into his jeans pocket and pulled out three crayons and a green colored pencil. His other pocket produced a piece of fools gold and an owl feather.

"Come on, Art." I glanced around the room to see if any of the teachers had left a pencil lying around.

Nothing.

"Oh, I know," Art reached up his sleeve and pulled out three pencils and a paintbrush. I grabbed one of the pencils and furiously brushed the eraser across my name while Bean did the same to Eric's.

The ninjas reappeared at the door, water-blasters cocked and ready.

Vinny let out a yelp and grabbed a handful of tests, holding them up in front of her face. The ninjas wouldn't dare squirt the tests.

"Get away from those tests!" The lead ninja jumped into the room, did a tornado kick, and knocked the tests out of Vinny's hands. The other ninjas rushed in after her.

"Run for it!" I yelled, dropping Eric's test.

Art reached for all the treasures he'd pulled from his pockets. The rest of us split up and headed out the door. One of the ninjas cartwheeled back to block our escape, but Bean and I got there first. Vinny dove between the ninja's spread legs and slid out into the hall behind us.

"Meet you at our secret hideout," I said, and we ran.

I sped down the A Hall. Breathing heavy. Slammed through the doors to the outside. Dashed around the school. Came back in the B Hall. Cut off into C Hall and stopped in front of the old janitor's closet. Gasping for breath.

Locked.

I reached my fingers through the crack under the door and slid the key out. A moment later I stepped inside.

The light from the hallway lit the closet just enough for me to find the string that hung down from the lightbulb in the center of the ceiling. I pulled the string and clicked the light on then closed the door and waited for the others.

A dusty old hall-waxing machine crouched in one corner, broken and useless. Empty bathroom-cleaner bottles lined a tilted shelf. It wasn't much of a secret hideout, but it was ours.

I slumped to the floor and wrapped my arms around my knees. Today stunk. First I got bees in my butt, then my mom discovered my math test, and then ninjas ruined the school. Water soaked me through and through. Worse, I hadn't gotten my name on Eric's paper.

Bean *thumped* through the door. "That was close," he said. "They almost got me."

Vinny slipped into the room and locked the door behind her. "They have Art."

My head shot up. "Oh no!"

"Yes." Vinny nodded. "The ninja leader caught him and dragged him to the principal's office. We all know there's no escape from there."

Chapter 11

A Plan

Art captured by the ninjas? I stood up and paced around our hideout. "We need a plan."

"Right. We've got to rescue Art." Bean slid a whiteboard out of its hiding place behind the waxer and uncapped a black marker. The marker's scent filled up the room and made my head fuzzy.

"Yes, but more than that. We've got to stop the ninjas. We can't let them have this school," Bean said.

"Right," Vinny agreed. "This is our school, and we're in charge here. We can't let the ninjas come in and ruin everything." She tapped her finger on her leg like clicking a computer mouse. That's what she does when she's thinking. "Why do you suppose the Majestic Order for Modern Schools picked Chrom-El to take over? It's loco. Wait a minute. Majestic Order for Modern Schools, M.O.M.S. It's an acronym."

"What?" Bean said.

"M.O.M.S." I said slowly. I remembered the mom out in the hall with the black fabric in her purse. A cold finger of surprise made me shiver. "I get it. Moms. The ninjas are the mothers of students in this school."

Vinny nodded. I told you there were a lot of moms who wanted to get their kids into the charter school but couldn't.

I stood up. "If they are moms and not real ninjas, then we can fight back."

"They outnumber us," Bean said. He drew a rough sketch of the school on the board, got out a red marker, and drew a dot for each of the ninjas. His picture looked more like a scribble. We needed Art for this kind of thing. Bean's smart, but his handwriting stinks.

I stared at the board. "You sure that's where the ninjas are right now?"

Bean shook his head. "That's where they were when I ran past, but they do move around. I'm pretty sure there are only a dozen or so, each armed with a water-blaster."

"Okay," I said, taking the marker from Bean and putting a black X on the board. "We're here. They're armed. We're not. We need weapons."

Vinny glanced around the closet and shook her head. "We've never been allowed to bring weapons to school. Perhaps we should start by getting rid of the ninjas' weapons."

"Good idea," I said. "How?"

The hideout fell silent for a few moments while we all tried to think.

"Those water-blasters are big, but they still only hold so much water," Vinny said. "They have to be refilled, or they're useless."

"So if they run out of water . . ." Bean smiled.

"They'll go to the sink and fill them back up." Vinny shook her head in frustration. "There's always more water."

"Not necessarily," I said.

"What do you mean?" Bean and Vinny said at the same time. "Jinx one-two-three-four—"

"Stop that!" I waved the marker for them to be quiet. "This is serious. We have to shut-off their water flow."

"You have an idea?" Bean asked.

"Our sink broke the other day, and my dad had to fix it. Before he started, he went downstairs and turned a lever that shut down the water to the entire house."

"You think there's a lever like that here at the school?" Vinny asked.

"There has to be. How else could Tom fix the plumbing?" I knew I was right.

"But where is it?" Bean asked.

"That's the question." I fiddled with the marker while my brain churned, looking for an answer. Then I had it. "There's a water meter hole out at the front of the school. You know that round metal plate in the grass?" I drew a circle on the white board where the meter was. "That means the water line must run into the school here." I drew a line into the front of the school. "And that's right about where the main janitor closet is at the front of the building, the one with the water heaters and furnace. The shut off valve has to be there."

"Perfect," Vinny said.

"Not quite. We still need weapons of our own. Something that will set the ninjas running and make them never want to come back," Bean said.

I let loose an evil laugh. "Remember several months ago at the high school basketball game?"

"Eeeew." Vinny's face turned green, and she looked like she might throw up. "That was so gross."

"Right. Someone put skunk oil in the air vents and made the whole school smell like a skunk's back end." I started laughing and couldn't stop for a moment. Then I remembered Art locked up in the principal's office.

"The police searched everywhere, right?" I edged over to the old floor waxer.

"Right," Bean said. "But they never caught the kids who did it."

I nodded with a big smile on my face.

"You didn't?" Vinny said, putting her hands on her hips.

"Of course not. But I was able to snatch the skunk oil from the high school kids who did. I think they planned to dump some in our vents too. Yucko."

I unlatched the side of the machine where you put the wax in and swung the compartment open. A little glass vial stood inside with a stopper shoved on tight and taped over for good measure.

"Brilliant," Bean and Vinny said together.

"Jinx," they both said, "one-two-three-four-five-six-seven-eight-nine-ten." Bean finished counting first. "You owe me your desert for lunch tomorrow."

Vinny groaned.

Bean grew silent and frowned at the skunk oil.

"What's wrong?" I asked.

"There isn't much oil left in that bottle. Even if you put it in the vents, I don't think it's enough to send the ninjas running." He rubbed his chin in thought.

"It might be enough to take out their leader though." I chuckled, took the tape off, and shoved the skunk oil in my pocket.

Vinny's eyes twinkled. "Great. I'd love to see that just as long as I don't have to smell it. But how do we get rid of the rest of the ninjas?"

A smile lit up Bean's face.

"Since you're smiling, you must have an idea," I said, handing the marker to Bean.

Chapter 12

Water-Blaster Science

Bean drew a picture of the insides of a water blaster on the white board. "It's just a matter of science. Water-blasters work by creating pressure inside the gun when you pump it. Then when you pull the trigger, the pressure forces the water to come shooting out. We could find a way to make our own water-blasters."

"Okay," I said. "We need some kind of plastic container that will hold water, some way to build up pressure inside, and some narrow thing for the water to come shooting out of."

I picked up one of the empty plastic cleaner bottles and took off the lid. The leftover smell from the toilet bowl cleaner made my eyes water.

"That won't do," I said.

"I've got it." Bean grinned. "Remember the other day when Art was playing basketball and dropped his water bottle. The water shot out all over the place."

"That's it, Bean," I said. "Squeezing a water bottle creates pressure which shoots the water out of the pop-top."

Vinny clapped her hands and smiled. "There are cases of bottled water in the lounge."

"Right," I said. "Enough that we won't have to fight alone."

"Who's going to help us?" Bean asked.

"I can think of a few people just off the top of my head. People who aren't very happy with the ninjas either. Mrs. Red and Principal Green for starters. In fact, I bet all the teachers and students would help us if we tell them what we have planned. The question is, how do we let them know?"

Vinny smiled, her eyes twinkling. "I can take care of that. The teachers' computers are all on instant messaging with Principal Green. I just need to sneak into the computer lab, reboot one of the computers, log on as Principal Green, and send out the message that we're going to stand and fight."

"You know the principal's password?" Bean and I said in disbelief.

"Sure," Vinny said. "Her log in is her name, and her password is her favorite color."

"Green!" we all shouted, then clapped our hands over our mouths as our shouts echoed in the small closet.

"Brilliant," Bean whispered.

"Gracias," Vinny said.

I frowned. Our plan was good, but not complete. "So we snag the water bottles and fight back," I said. "But Art's still locked up in the office. Someone has to rescue him."

They both looked at me, eyes wide.

"I can't do it." Vinny shuddered. "I have to send the message from the computer lab."

"Right, and I came up with the water bottle idea," Bean said. "I should be the one to get them from the Teachers' Lounge and pass them out."

"I guess that leaves me," I said, rubbing my sweaty hands on my jeans. "The office isn't far from the janitor's closet where the water line is. I can shut down their ammo and then go after the ninja leader and free Art."

"Great," Vinny and Bean said. Both looked relieved that I'd taken the most dangerous job.

"Right," I said. Bees swarmed around in my gut. I took a shaky breath. "That's it then. Let's go."

We gave each other the Smartboys' high five then unlocked the door and split up.

Chapter 13

Trapped

The halls stood empty. Lunchtime had ended, and everyone had gone back to class—except us, of course. I crept down the hall, fear pumping through me. I had to face the ninja leader. Be brave like Beowulf, I told myself.

My hands shook as I marched past the classrooms. Most of the doors were closed, but the one to our own room was open. I edged to the door and peeked inside. Everyone's heads were down while they wrote in their math workbooks.

I slid past the door and ran the rest of the way to the janitor's closet at the front of the school. Gasping for breath, I twisted the door handle, hoping it wasn't locked. The door opened a crack, and I slipped inside.

"Monkey?" Tom Brown sloshed the mop in the bucket he'd just filled with water.

I jumped in surprise.

"What are you doing here?" Tom said. He looked puzzled but didn't seem angry.

Tom and I get along pretty well. We have ever since the Smartboys helped him come up with a good way of getting graffiti off the bathroom walls.

"This school's in trouble," I told him.

"I agree with you there," he said. "Water everywhere. People slipping in the halls. Someone's going to get hurt."

Tom cares a lot about safety.

"It's the ninjas," I said. "We have to stop them."

"That's why you're out of class?"

"Sure is."

"You got a plan?"

"Yep. First thing we have to do is shut off the main water line so the ninjas can't refill their guns."

"Good thinking," Tom said. He wiggled his way behind the furnace. I heard a squeal and then a *kathunk*. He came back out and wiped his hands on his overalls. "Now what?"

I grimaced. "Leave the rest to me."

I crossed the hall to the office and peeked in the window. The room appeared empty, but a closer look showed Art's silhouette behind Principal Green's door. Goose bumps prickled my arms. I wondered where the ninja leader had gone. She couldn't have left Art in there alone.

Mrs. Red came down the hall carrying several cases of bottled water. She set one outside each classroom door.

"You're being very naughty, Monkey," she whispered as she passed me.

I smiled at her. She doesn't call me Monkey very often. As soon as she turned the corner, I slipped into the office. That just left one more door between Art and me. I tiptoed across the main office and jerked open Principal Green's door.

"Come on," I hissed, motioning for Art to come out.

"No," he mouthed, waving his hand. "Go away."

"It's all right, Art. Come on." I ran over to him.

His eyes bugged out, and a moan escaped him. I whirled around to see what he was looking at. The lead ninja stood less than a foot away, her red water-blaster pointed in my face.

"Thank you, Kyung-sam. You may go now," she said.

Looking miserable, Art slipped out of the office, and the ninja closed the door with a loud *thump*.

Chapter 14

The World's Biggest Water Fight

I gulped and licked my lips.

Only the ninja's piercing brown eyes showed through her mask. She motioned to the desk. There sat two tests, nameless, one with red marks all over it, one neat and clean except for a thumbprint smudge on one edge. My test and Eric's. An open ink pad sat next to the papers.

"Johnny Lovebird," the ninja said. "Just the boy I wanted. Please, press your thumb onto the ink pad and make a print right there on the paper next to the other one."

My heart thundered in my ears. I'd been so stupid, leaving a thumbprint like that. As soon as she got the match, she'd have proof of how smart I was. My gut twisted with fear. I looked around the room. But no ancient, giant-forged sword lay on top of Principal Green's inbox. Things like that only show up in stories. I eased my hand into my pocket. Good thing I'd brought my own weapon along.

The ninja stepped closer. A pearl of water dripped from the end of the blaster. Sweat trickled down the back of my neck as I eased the stopper out of the vial.

"Listen," I said. "I think you must have me mistaken for someone else. I never get good grades. You . . . you need Eric Dripp. I'm sure you'll find that's his thumbprint there on the good test paper."

"I don't think so," the ninja said. "I believe you are a smart boy, Johnny. You can't hide it any longer. I know."

"N-n-no," I said backing away from the desk. A sharp pain stabbed through my gut.

Bbbffpptbbffpptbbffppt!

The bees exploded in an angry swarm, filling the small office with unbearable stink.

"That does it," the ninja cried, pinching her nose. "No more Mexican food for you, Johnny."

I sucked in a surprised breath. Only one mom in the whole world knew what I'd eaten for dinner last night. All the pieces clicked together in my brain. Mom's new class at the Fitness Center must be karate. She'd bruised her knuckles while learning to break boards. And this morning she'd figured out what I'd done on my math quiz.

She grabbed my hand out of my pocket and forced it toward the ink pad. Too bad for her I had the open vial of skunk oil in my hand. It slipped from my fingers, hit the floor and shattered, sending skunk oil flying.

I jumped back just in time to avoid it.

Mom wasn't fast enough. The skunk oil sprayed all over her pants.

"Aaaaaahhhh!!!" she screamed. "Johnny Lovebird, you're grounded for the rest of your life."

While my mom was still in shock, I pressed my thumb against the inkpad and then smeared the ink across the thumbprint already on the paper, obliterating it. Then I bolted into the main office.

Mom tried to grab me, but I dodged away and hit the switch to turn on the announcement system. "Attack!" I yelled. My voice carried over the speakers to every classroom. I raced from the office before my mom could get a hold of me. My brain spun like a tornado. I never imagined my mom would turn ninja and take over a school. Crazy.

She chased me down the hall.

Doors flew open. Kids and teachers grabbed the water bottles, popped open the lids and turned them on the ninjas. Sprays of water erupted around me.

The ninjas screamed and pumped their water-blasters, sending torrents of water back at the students. The kids shouted and ducked into their classrooms. Their faces appeared around the door just long enough to shoot more water at the ninjas.

One of the ninjas did a cartwheel and kicked the water bottles out of the kids' hands.

Principal Green charged down the hall right into the spray of water-blasters. Her dry-clean only shirt got soaked instantly. Bellowing, she dumped a whole pitcher of ice water over two of the ninjas' heads.

The ninjas shrieked and raced back to the bathroom to refill their water-blasters. I saw their faces peeking out as I ran past.

"Ha!" I shouted. "It's over. You have no more water."

Three more ninjas came down the hall toward me. Cold water sprayed in my face. I guess they hadn't wasted all their water in the first round of fighting. I slipped and fell on my behind. Out of the corner of my eye I saw Tom uselessly trying to mop up all the water before someone got hurt. Too late for me.

Mom grabbed me by the shoulders, dragged me up, and pinned me to the wall.

"Look what you've done," she cried. "You've ruined everything." Tears formed in her eyes, or water from a half dozen water bottles that sprayed her from angry students trying to help get me free.

A wet sponge flew past behind her back. A ninja deflected it with a crescent kick then squirted a pair of first graders on their pants so it looked like they had wet themselves. The first graders burst into tears and raced away.

"Oh no you don't!" A gang of sixth graders raced into the hall and skidded to a stop, spraying the ninjas. The ninjas tried to stop the water with their arms, but the water *splooshed* past and hit them in the face.

Ignoring the battle, the lead ninja held me tight, her fingers digging into my shoulders.

"Mom," I gasped. "Why did you do this?"

"Because I know you're smart, Johnny. I just know you are, and your teacher refuses to see it. You keep getting bad grades, and think-times, and it's not right. You're probably the smartest boy in this school."

Her shoulders shook, so I knew she was crying. I didn't tell her that Bean thought of using Pi, proving he was smarter than I am. The skunk smell wafted from her and scared the bees in my butt into silence.

Out of ammo, the other ninja moms raced past us, heading for the school's front door. Dozens of kids chased after them, shouting and spraying them with water.

"Mom, I don't want anyone to know I'm smart, okay? They'll send me away to that Gifted Program, and I want to stay here with Bean and Vinny and my other friends. I like this school."

Mom let go of my shoulders and stepped back. "But Johnny, it's such a waste. If you got in the Gifted

Program, you could learn so much more. You could get into college early and graduate at the top of your class, and become a world famous scientist or something." The tears shimmered in her eyes. "You're my son, and I want the very best for you."

I lowered my head and stared at my shoes. I didn't want to disappoint my mother, but I didn't want to leave my friends either. I had to think of something fast.

"Mom," I said, taking her hand. "I'm smart enough I don't need a Gifted Program. I learn stuff better on my own. If you let me stay here, I promise I'll study really hard and make you proud of me. Besides, I want to be a famous author when I grow up, not a scientist. Bean's the science guru."

Mom's eyes scrunched up for a moment then she dragged me into a great big hug. That hug felt good, except I had a hard time keeping my legs away from the skunk oil on her pants.

Then she let me go. "Okay, Johnny. We'll try it your way."

"My friends call me Monkey," I said, wiping the water out of my eyes.

"Right, Monkey." She tousled my hair and walked out of the school, trying not to slip on the wet floor.

Chapter 15

Secrets

Bean, Art, and Vinny raced up to me, holding empty water bottles. Vinny's wet black hair stuck to her face. Water dripped from Bean's pants. Only Art seemed to have stayed dry. Pools of water covered the floor, with Tom mopping furiously to clean up the deluge.

"You okay, Monkey?" Art asked. His face twisted in shame. "I'm real sorry about getting you trapped in the office."

"I'm fine," I said, attempting to wipe my face dry with my wet shirtsleeve. "It wasn't your fault." I had a funny taste in my mouth after talking to my mom.

No. It wasn't Art's fault. It was mine. I started this whole mess because I'd done my math quiz wrong. I shuddered. From now on, I'd have to do my schoolwork right. But I vowed that wouldn't keep me from learning a bunch of stuff on my own.

"So," Bean said. "Did you get the skunk oil on the ninja leader?"

I nodded, feeling a bit guilty about that.

"Did you see who she was? Did you get her mask off?"

Uh-oh. I didn't want to tell them that my own mother had been responsible for all the horrible things the ninjas had done. She had agreed to keep my secret identity safe. I figured I'd better do the same for her.

"I didn't get her mask off. Never saw her face."

"No problem," Vinny said. "All we have to do is find the mom that smells like a skunk, and then she'll be in big trouble."

They laughed.

I laughed with them and made a note to myself not to invite anyone over to my house until the smell had worn off. "Come on. Let's go help Tom clean up this mess."

"Right." Bean splashed across the floor to the janitor closet to get a mop. The rest of us followed.

"You know," Art said, pretending to dribble a basketball and shoot a swisher. "That was great. We creamed those ninjas. Smartboys ten, ninjas zero!" His face glowed with excitement. "They should make water fighting an Olympic sport."

The rest of us laughed and did a high five. "Smartboys Rule!" We shouted together.

Smartboys
Club
Secret Notebook

Warning!
If you read this
you might get smart

read
at your
own risk!

Right
You have
been
Warned ⌀

Club motta: Learning is

NOTES   Fun!

Members

Monkey
Bean
Art
Vinny

Smartboys Rule!

Bean stop
doing math
on the members
page

Hey Art
was
drawing

200
51
75
199
12
537

90

The digestive system
or what causes farts!

you eat
beans

mouth

Swallow → esophagus

But beans don't break down well.

Digestive enzymes break down food.

Stomach

Large intestine →

Small intestine

Beans enter large intestine. Bacteria breaks down the beans into gases.
Methane, hydrogen, hydrogen sulfide

beans enter small intestine more digestion. Beans still fighting back.

↑
That's the Smelly stuff

gas comes out. stinging like bees.

eeeeeew!

Gross!

91

Weather

Weather is caused by the heating and cooling of the earth's surface and atmosphere.

Clouds:

cirrus —

stratus —

cumulus —

cumulonimbus —

Hot air rises ↗ Cold air sinks ↘ that's what makes wind!

Water evaporates into the air to make clouds, rain, and snow.

Hygrometer - measures humidity
thermometer - measures temperature
barometer - measures air pressure
anemometer - measures wind speed

Changes in temperature, air pressure, humidity, and wind signal a change in weather.

Beowulf

The story of Beowulf is over one thousand two hundred years old.

It's written in Old English.

Heald þu nu, hruse,
nu hæleð ne mostan.

you call this English?

(modern English) Hold them now, Earth,
now hand of man cannot.

(based on F. Klaeber's translation)

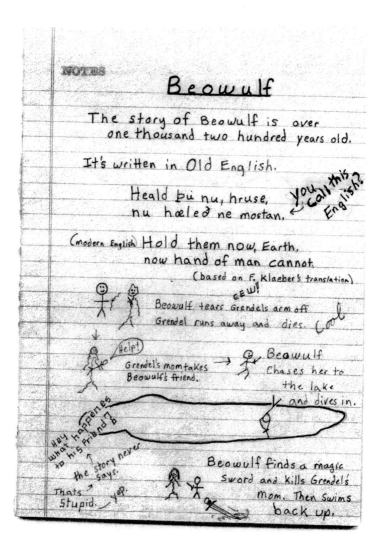

EEW!

Beowulf tears Grendels arm off
Grendel runs away and dies. *cool*

Help!

Grendel's mom takes
Beowulf's friend.

Beowulf
chases her to
the lake
and dives in.

Hey what happened to his friend?

the story never says.

Thats stupid. *yep.*

Beowulf finds a magic
sword and kills Grendel's
mom. Then swims
back up.

Algebra

▮ ▮ + ? = 5

Bean and I go to the store and buy 5 candy bars. Vinny sees I have two candy bars and asks how many Bean has. He won't tell. I say we bought 5.

Vinny writes what she knows. then she uses a letter for what she doesn't know.

$$2 + C = 5$$

c for candy bars

= means both sides are the same. She can change one side if she does the same on the other.

$$2 + C = 5$$
$$-2 \qquad -2$$
$$0 + C = 3$$

$$C = 3$$

Now she knows that Bean has 3 candy bars.

That's how algebra works.

and me!

and he better share with me!

Pi (π)

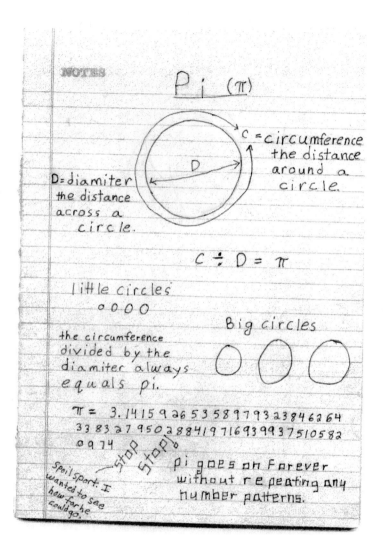

C = circumference
the distance
around a
circle.

D = diamiter
the distance
across a
circle.

$$C \div D = \pi$$

little circles
o o o o

Big circles

the circumference
divided by the
diamiter always
equals pi.

π = 3.14159 26 53 58 97 93 23 84 62 64
33 83 27 950 28 84 19 71 69 39 93 75 10 58 2
09 74

stop Stop!

pi goes on Forever
without repeating any
number patterns.

Spoil sport. I
wanted to see
how far he
could go.

95

That's where I draw the line!
(This is where I stand and fight no matter what)

The ALAMO mission   San Antonio Texas

February and
March 1836

Colonel Travis
and less than 200
Freedom fighters.

Mexican General
Santa Anna and his
Huge Army.

Colonel Travis tells his men if they stay and fight, they'll all die. They can't win. But if they can hold out long enough their friend, Sam Houston, could gather an army big enough to keep Santa Anna from capturing Texas.

Whoever will stand and fight step over the line!

Colonel Travis draws a line with his sword in the sand. All but one guy step over the line.

Colonel Travis and his freedom fighters hold out for 13 days before Santa Anna takes the Alamo and kills them all.
Sam Houston gathers an army and drives Santa Anna back to mexico!

96

Mass and Momentum

mass × velocity
= momentum

mass is all the books
plus the cart

cart with
books going
down hill to
the dumpster

Velocity is
speed
in this
direction

$m × v = m_0$

Tons of books going fast = momentum.

Newtons First Law: Things in motion tend
to stay in Motion!

Art throws the rock which
stops the Cart

momentum
makes the
books fly
Forward.

This is you if you
don't wear a
seatbelt in a
car!

Coach Delamar
says "keep your throwing
arm over your head and
step toward the target"
when you throw the ball.
(or rock in this case.)

How water blasters work!

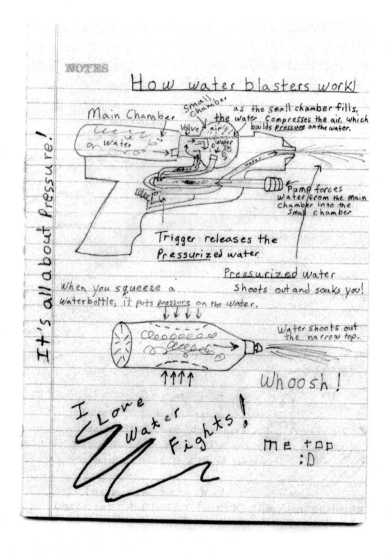

It's all about pressure!

Main Chamber

Small Chamber

as the small chamber fills, the water compresses the air, which builds pressure on the water.

Valve   air

water

water

Pump forces water from the main chamber into the small chamber

Trigger releases the Pressurized water.

Pressurized water shoots out and soaks you!

When you squeeze a waterbottle, it puts pressure on the water.

Water shoots out the narrow top.

Whoosh!

I Love Water Fights!

ME too :D

About The Author

Rebecca Shelley loves adventuring and spent a lot of time in her youth doing things like dog sledding, hiking, camping, horseback riding, and even sky diving. She has a special fondness for dragons and fairies and wrote her first book in Elementary School. To learn more or to get printable copies of the Secret Notebook, visit her website at www.rebeccashelley.com.

Books by Rebecca Shelley

Smartboys Club
Book 1: Bees in My Butt
Book 2: We Flushed it Down the Potty
Book 3: I Took A Burp
Book 4: I Lost My Head
Book 5: My Stomach Explodes
Book 6: All I Got for Christmas

Firebird
Young Aedus of the Nanuk Clan knows nothing of the war between the spirits or the Firebird. Aedus wants only to prove himself a man in the Great Hunt. But when the battling spirits threaten to destroy his clan, he risks everything—not just his life, but his very humanity—to save his people.

Black Dragon
Twelve-year-old Weldon is a gifted artist, but when his drawings of fairies and dragons come to life, he finds himself caught between some deadly criminals and the jewels they want. Only his dedication and imagination can save him and his friends.

Mist Warriors
The mist on Lake Tahoe holds powerful and dangerous secrets. When Robby's sister vanishes into the mist, Robby follows and finds himself entangled in an ancient struggle between magical foes.

Ebon Blade (coming soon)
A ragged street boy named Brian snatches a cursed blade that thrusts him into a bloody war of succession. The blade carries a dark magic that makes Brian a dangerous fighter, but in the process it takes control of his mind and spirit. He finds he must choose between his own freedom and the power to save his friends.

Firebird (Sneak Peek)

The Beathan army swept past Aedus toward the Morag. Asgeir stayed at Aedus's side. The fury of the two armies clashing together rocked the ground beneath Aedus's feet. The spirits of the Beathan and the Morag moved so fast, Aedus couldn't see the battle, just flashes of light and dark.

Beathan screams twisted in the air with the howls and shrieks of the Morag. Aedus lost sight of the clan camp in the spinning mass of warring spirits.

A black wave of Morag broke through the front line and surged toward Aedus. Reflexively Aedus drew a ward in the air, knowing it would have little effect, the full might of the Beathan already stood around him.

Asgeir leaped in front of him, and sank his spear into a giant raven. The raven let out a horrible screech and clawed at Asgeir.

Asgeir twisted around, hurling the bird off his spear away from him. The Morag changed from a giant raven into a mountain cat and leaped back toward Aedus. Again Asgeir drove it away.

"You speared it," Aedus said in shock to Asgeir, who was locked in battle with another black spirit. "But it didn't die. It just changed forms and came back."

"Kill it?" Asgeir shouted. "Think boy. How do you kill something that has no mortal form?"

A bright wave of Beathan spun past Aedus, catching the Morag that had broken through and forcing them back away from Aedus's protectors. Aedus gasped. In the screams and raging battle that swirled around him, he recognized a pattern.

The Morag seemed intent on breaking through the Beathan to get to him.

"The clan!" Aedus screamed, sprinting toward the camp. If the Morag were after him, they'd be after the rest of the clan as well, but the Beathan all fought around Aedus.

"No!" Asgeir grabbed the back of his shirt and jerked him to a stop. "We must keep the battle away from the clan."

"But won't the Morag attack them?"

The spirits spun around him faster and faster. The wind of their passing tore at his clothes and whipped his hair into his eyes.

"The Morag don't care about the clan right now. It's you they want." Aedus could barely hear Asgeir's shout above the rushing Beathan and Morag.

Again and again the Morag broke through, and the Beathan spun past, carrying them away.

"Me?" Aedus gasped. "Why?" The speed of the battle sucked the air from him, making it hard to breathe.

A wave of Morag broke through the Beathan defenses and lunged at Aedus, drowning out Asgeir's answer.

Asgeir and the other four who had stayed beside Aedus sprang into action, stabbing, spinning, kicking doing everything they could to keep the circle of black creatures away from Aedus.

One of the Morag transformed into the shape of a ferret and scrambled between Asgeir's legs while Asgeir fought with two others.

Aedus swept his arms up, forming a ward as the ferret twisted into the black bear who had led the charge.

The bear let out a low growl and lunged at Aedus.

Aedus stepped back and formed a second ward and a third even as the bear shattered the first.

"You're too weak," the bear growled, advancing slowly, savoring the fear he must smell from Aedus. He pawed the second ward aside.

Aedus took another step back and formed a fourth ward between himself and the bear.

A sharp pain raked Aedus's side. A wildcat had leaped on him from behind, sinking its claws into him. The bear let out a booming laugh as Aedus twisted away.

Asgeir leaped on the cat's back, strangling it with his spear.

Aedus staggered to his knees, pressing his hand against the deep wound. Blood flowed between his fingers.

The black bear swiped aside Aedus's last two wards, and closed in for the final kill.

"No!" Aedus screamed, crossing his arms over his chest and then swinging them out to his sides like he'd done in the storm with Keane. Even as he did it, he heard Keane's voice in the back of his mind.

Not that ward. Never, never do that again. Keane had said it was the ward to call the Firebird, and the Firebird always brought death.

Fire lit the air, enveloping Aedus in flames. Aedus swung his hands forward, sending the flames straight into the bear's chest.

The black bear twisted into human form and let out an earsplitting scream. The ground shook. Beathan and Morag alike combined into one violent spinning mass of air.

Lightning split the sky.